The Adventures of Nogard and Jackpot

by Alan F. Beck

SKNAHT,
A Beck

2022

Alan F. Beck
alanfbeck@earthlink.net
www.alanfbeck.com

Dedication:
To Bonnie,
who put up with me these many years.

To Jasmine, Tovah and Talia,
who let me see the wonder of the world through young eyes again.

The Adventures of Nogard and Jackpot

Written and illustrated by
Alan F. Beck

Jackpot was bored.
Her owners were away.
She was bored.
She was really bored.
She was really, really bored.

Then one day she heard a noise.
It was coming from the closet.

A tiny voice calling
"Olleh, olleh"?

"Olleh," thought Jackpot.
What does that mean?

She opened the closet door looked inside.
Way in the back next to an mirror she saw a little
dragon inside an old shoe.

"Olleh" it said.
"Olleh? Oh you mean hello," said Jackpot.

"Who are you?" asked Jackpot.

"Nogard," the dragon said.
"Nogard?" said Jackpot".
"That's a funny name."

The little dragon climbed out of the shoe and Jackpot saw a note tied to Nogard's tail.

It said:

Now it turned out that Nogard was a rascally little dragon.
He had his own funny backward language and he liked to explore and play games.

Jackpot looked the note again.
"Are you hungry?" asked Jackpot.
"Ton tey," said Nogard. "Yalp etarip!"

" Ton tey?" "Yalp etarip?" thought Jackpot.

"Oh," said Jackpot. "I get it."
"Not yet, play pirate."

Nogard nodded his head yes.
He took off, ran in to the den
and climbed up on the desk.
He made a pirate hat out of a
tissue and drew a treasure map
on the piece of paper.

Then he made an X on the map to mark
the spot where he thought the treasure of
food was hidden.

Nogard sniffed in the air.
He jumped up and shouted
"Wollof em!"

He hopped off the desk and ran outside into the garden.
"Oh, you mean follow me," said Jackpot and she followed him
out of the back door.

"Tae?" asked Nogard.
"Do you mean eat?"
"You can't eat that. That's a flower," said Jackpot.

He picked up a
long, slippery thing.
"Tae?" asked Nogard.
"No, that's a worm."

They ran back inside the house and stopped
at the fish bowl.
"Tae?" asked Nogard.
"No, that's Larry, our pet fish."

Then they raced into the kitchen.

"Do you see any food?" asked Jackpot.
"Sey I od." shouted Nogard.
"I see, you mean,' yes I do.'"

First Nogard found
a bowl of noodles.

"Muy," said Nogard.

"Oh, you mean yum,"
said Jackpot.

Then he saw some
cocoa.

"Muy," said Nogard.

He found some cookies.

"Muy, muy, muy," said Nogard.

After lunch they decided to take a nap.

Nogard found a
quilted pot holder
and crawled under.

When they woke up an hour later,
it was time to play again.

First they played a game of leap frog.

Nogard found a Jack-o-lantern made out of a pumpkin.

They built a tiny snowman.

Then played with some funny eye-glasses.

Nogard found some sticky paste and papers.

And made Jackpot a Valentine.

They discovered a basket of
yarn to play in.

Later, Nogard painted a picture of Jackpot.

Nogard showed Jackpot how he could float in the air.

"That's so neat," thought Jackpot.

They played all day.

But now it was getting dark and time for bed.

Nogard ran off.

Jackpot found him in the kitchen taking a bath in her water bowl.

"You rascal," Jackpot said.

Nogard asked, "Peels won?"

"Yes." Jackpot said, "Sleep now."

"But first you have to brush your teeth."

"Muy," said Nogard.

"No, no," said Jackpot.
"Don't eat it. Just brush and don't swallow."

"Daer a yrots?" asked Nogard.

"Okay," Jackpot said, "Read me a story."

So Nogard read a story to Jackpot so fast that she didn't understand a single word. It seems Nogard didn't know how to read anyway.

"Derit," yawned Nogard.
"I am tired too," said Jackpot.

Jackpot gave her new friend a good night kiss.

"Sknaht," said Nogard. "I dah nuf."
"I had fun too," said Jackpot.

They both layed down on Jackpot's pillow and went to sleep.

In the morning, Nogard was gone.

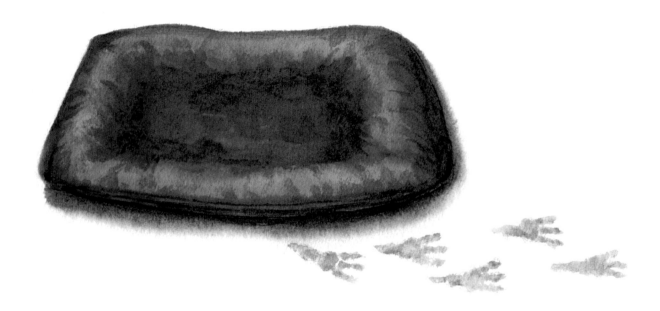

Jackpot searched and searched, but she could not find him.

She went to the closet and saw footprints leading up to the mirror. There was a message written on the mirror glass. It said,
Thanks for taking care of Nogard.
He had a great day.
Nogard's mom.

Then something was shaking her shoulder.
"Wake up. Wake up you sleepy head.
Miss Jackie Potts, it's time for you to get up.
Breakfast is ready."

"Okay, Mom," Jackie said.

Jackie yawned and rubbed the sleep from her eyes.

She looked around her room and saw the morning sun shining through the window.

Jackie thought about her dream
and wondered…

Was that toothpaste on her toy dragon's nose?

"Muy," Jackie said.

And then she smiled.

THE END

Made in the USA
Middletown, DE
17 October 2022

12504615R00020